Small

By Tim Winton

Tim Winton

Small Mercies

PICADOR SHOTS

First published 2006 by Picador
an imprint of Pan Macmillan Ltd
Pan Macmillan, 20 New Wharf Road, London N1 9RR
Basingstoke and Oxford
Associated companies throughout the world
www.panmacmillan.com

ISBN-13: 978-0-330-44574-0
ISBN-10: 0-330-44574-X

1 3 5 7 9 8 6 4 2

A CIP catalogue record for this book is available from
the British Library.

Typeset by Intype Libra Ltd
Printed and bound in Great Britain by
Mackays of Chatham plc, Chatham, Kent

PETER DYSON CAME HOME one day to find his wife dead in the garage. He'd only been gone an hour, kicking a ball in the park with their four-year-old son. The Ford's motor was still running, its doors locked, and even before he knew it for certain, before he put the sledge-hammer through the window, before the ambulance crew confirmed it, he was grateful to her for sparing the boy.

He held himself together until the funeral and then for a few weeks he lost his mind. His mates avoided him, but their wives rallied to save him. He drank alone until he blacked out. When he bothered to eat he forked up food straight from the casserole dishes his friends' wives left him when they dropped Ricky back in the evenings. One morning he woke beside one of those wives and she was weeping.

Thereafter Dyson endeavoured, for the sake of his son, to lead a decent, stable, predictable existence, something as close to normal as a ruined man could manage. Though he hated the house now and the city around it, he was determined to stay on in Fremantle for Ricky's sake, so that his year of kindergarten might proceed uninterrupted.

And somehow the better part of a year fell by. Ricky smiled, unbidden, and seemed to forget his mother for weeks at a time. It was a mercy. Dyson worked a couple of days a week. He did not see friends, he wasn't sure he had any left. His life was not joyless yet its pleasures were close to theoretical. He appreciated more than he felt. Still, he believed that he was making progress. He was not reconciled but he was recovering.

What undid him was not the approaching anniversary of his wife's death but the onset of winter. He was, quite suddenly, overtaken by disgust.

All it took was a change in the wind. He hated winter. The first major cold front of the season was heralded by the usual blustering nor'wester, a wind that always seemed used up and clammy, too eerily warm for what lay behind it, but this gusting breeze was especially dirty because Dyson woke early to the terrible stink of sheep. Being a country boy, he wasn't particularly sensitive to the smell of livestock. But this was the concentrated urinal stench of thousands of merinos being stacked in a floating high-rise. Down on the docks they were loading live cargo for the Saudis. Rising to pull down the window sash he found that the odour was in the curtains already. Outside on the line, the damp washing was tainted. The whole town was overtaken.

At breakfast Ricky wanted to know where the stink came from. There was no point in keeping the sordid details from him. They'd have to pass the ships on the way to kindy anyway and he'd see for himself how they jammed them in tier upon tier. He told the boy about the weeks the animals spent at sea and the awful heat and the mortality rates and how the knives awaiting them at the other end must come as cruel relief after such an ordeal. Ricky grew silent. Dyson regretted his frankness. Neither of them could finish breakfast for the smell of death in the house. Dyson helped the boy dress and afterwards, trying to shave, he began to shake. He suddenly knew there was no way he was going down into that garage this morning. Even if he could make himself roll up the door and start the car, the smell of monoxide would set him off. You couldn't trust yourself to drive in that sort of state, not with a child in the car. The whole business was suddenly at the back of his throat; he was brimming.

Ricky enjoyed the taxi ride. Dyson smiled for him despite the sick smell of the driver's sweat and the oppressive babble of FM radio blasting into him from behind. When the boy was safely delivered, Dyson got out at the public pool whose sun-shades and pennants snapped and lurched in the mounting gale.

The pool was a grim morning ritual. The point was supposed to be to lose weight and regain some fitness but the real benefit lay in the monotony of swimming laps. For half an hour every morning, while he hauled himself through the water, he went mercifully blank. He preferred this time of day because the initial rush was over, the wiry execs and hairy machos were gone and the average lap speed was less frenetic. Mothers, retirees and a few shy students swam without hounding each other up the lanes.

But this morning the changerooms seemed unaccountably damp. Their pungent cocktail of bleach and mildew made his head spin. Even the pool water felt wrong; it was soupy and the chlorine made him gag. On his first lap every breath tasted of sheep piss. It was a relief to feel the distracting chill of wind-driven rain on his back.

He always liked the way the pool rendered the plainest body handsome. It cheered him to see the fat become stately and the aged graceful. Today, in an effort to break this dangerous mood, he concentrated on the feet kicking ahead of him and the pearly bubbles that trailed in their wake. Lap after lap he found himself behind a woman whose toenails were lacquered a kind of burgundy. It was the colour that initially caught his attention. There was something luscious about it. He became mesmerized by the symmetry of the woman's toes and then by the delicate veins that stood out in the high arches of her feet which, against the chemical blue of the pool, were as white and comely as those of any classical statue.

He crawled along, bewitched in the woman's wake. She was a good swimmer. Her legs were strong. As she churned through the water ahead of him he watched the movement of her calves, her working thighs and the mound of her buttocks. She was beautiful. He loved her belly in the nylon sheath of her Speedo suit and the way her breasts moulded to her. The water he swam in became turbulent. Without realizing it, he'd sped up until the woman's feet were almost striking him in the face and when he backed off he lost rhythm. Dyson tried to shift his attention from the swimmer ahead by taking an interest in people passing in other lanes, but it was no better. They were, all of them, lithe and delicious. He had a perilous urge to reach out and touch smooth limbs, to lay his cheek, his ear, his lips against every firm belly. Each new swimmer, male and female, was more beautiful than the one before and he swam without really breathing for fear of interrupting this view of perfection until his stroke became ragged and the air he was forced to gulp tasted foul. Blots and sparks rose behind his eyes and he blundered, gagging, against the lane rope to hang there like a piece of snagged trash.

When he had recovered somewhat, the sky was dirty-dark above him. As they climbed from the pool his fellow swimmers regained their varicose veins and moles and hanging guts. The sudden ugliness of everything was crushing. He felt a poisonous surge of revulsion towards everything around him but nothing disgusted him more than himself.

During his final punitive sprint to the wall, the water around him was all Band-Aids, floating scabs and hanks of hair. He was roiling through sweat and spit and other people's piss and when he hoisted himself out, the air was just as brothy.

On all fours, dripping and panting until he began to sob and cause people to step around him in consternation, he knew that things were wrong, that he had to make a change. Everything here was tainted now. Continuing to pretend otherwise was simply and finally beyond him.

In the spring Dyson packed up and moved south. He took possession of his mother's house on the hill above the harbour in Angelus. He knocked out a wall and painted the rest in colours that would have made his mother blanch. The roof was fair, the foundations good and being home gave him a sense of satisfaction that might once have alarmed him. He was not blind to the irony of starting over in a house and a community he'd long ago left behind, but it was a ready and practical option and it was the least disruptive for Ricky who seemed to love the place. Right at the outset Dyson sensed how much less force of will it took for him to be himself in front of his son and this new ease seemed to relax the boy. He'd never seen so clearly how this worked, how the boy took his emotional cues from him. He couldn't imagine what he'd done to the kid already without realizing it. He had to think of the future and to seem happy with their new start.

Although Ricky was enrolled at a kindergarten an easy walk from the house, Dyson kept him home for the first week of term so they could explore the old town together and he could give the kid his bearings. They walked the white beaches and hiked over the granite bluffs that dominated the harbour. From a windswept lookout, staring south across the whitecapped open ocean, they tried to picture the ice, the penguins, the very bottom of the world. Back at home Ricky passed nails while Dyson built him a cubbyhouse between the peppermints in the backyard. In the evenings, for as long as they could stand the cold, clean wind, they watched the lights of ships track through the narrow entrance to the encircling harbour. Rain chattered on the roof at night as father and son lay spooned together in bed.

For a day or so Ricky was fascinated by the

idea that this was once his grandmother's house. He was so young when she died that he didn't really remember her but he insisted on seeing photographs, especially those few with him and his grandmother together. Dyson dreaded the photo albums but let the boy thumb through them, enthralled. Within the hour, Ricky had moved on to some fresh enthusiasm. He was small for his age, a serious dark-eyed child, curious and rarely fearful. Dyson himself had been, he gathered, much like him. He treasured the boy for selfish reasons. Ricky was the only thing that offered his life any meaning. He couldn't bear to think what damage the past year had done him.

In the days after poring over the photos, Ricky seemed more tender and solicitous. It was as though he finally understood that they were both motherless. Their Lego projects were quiet affairs. They sat at the table in the weak afternoon light with only the companionable scratch of pencils passing between them.

Dyson began to think about getting a job. For years he taught woodwork and outdoor ed, but after Ricky was born and the depression took hold of Sophie, he spent so much time on leave that he had to resign. So many emergencies, hospitalizations, sleepless nights. When things were stable he operated as a mobile handyman. The flexible hours allowed him to be around to pick up the debris when things unravelled at home. But it was fifteen months since he'd worked at all and he'd come south without any solid idea of what he might do for a job down here. It wasn't a matter of urgent concern. He owned this house and the place up in the city was let, so he didn't need much money. A job was more about adding some shape to his new life, meeting people he could start from scratch with, free from pity or recrimination. It would all have to be new. There was no point in seeking out people he'd gone to school with a decade ago. It was a small town but hopefully not so small that you couldn't choose your company.

The day he got Ricky settled into kindy, he took a walk down the main street with a view to wandering along the wharves to think about his prospects. He was barely halfway to the docks when a woman called his name.

Peter Dyson! cried a tall grey-haired woman in her sixties. It *is* you!

She stood in the doorway of a newsagency with a girl of seven or so whose lank blonde hair fretted in the wind.

Mrs Keenan?

Marjorie, she said with mock sternness. You're not a boy anymore.

How are you? he asked.

Gobsmacked. Don't just stand there, boy. Come and give me a hug. I don't believe it!

Dyson stepped up and embraced her for a moment. He'd almost forgotten what another adult body felt like. For a moment he found it difficult to speak.

Look at you, she said. Just look at you.

He managed to laugh. Marjorie Keenan was still sprightly but her face was lined. She seemed older than she was.

And what brings you back to town? she asked, composing herself and pulling the child gently into her hip.

Oh, life I spose. I've moved into Mum's place.

I don't believe it! she declared with delight.

Well, neither did I. But there we are.

Come for dinner. Don'd love to see you.

Maybe I will some time.

Bring your family.

That'd be nice.

You know that I'll keep you to it, she said with a smile.

I don't doubt it for a minute.

Dyson looked at the little girl who chewed her lip.

This is our Sky, said Marjorie Keenan.

Hello, said Dyson.

I'll chase you up, said the old woman.

Dyson laughed and stepped back into the street. He headed down to the town jetty with a creeping sense of disquiet. It was the child, Sky. Of course it was possible that she was a neighbour's daughter or one of the many strays of the sort he used to meet at the Keenans' himself when he was a schoolboy. They were warm, kind people, Don and Marjorie, and their place was often a haven for runaways or foster kids, the beneficiaries of one church mission or other. Sky had the shop-soiled look of one of those children. But the dirty-blonde hair and the way she clung to Marjorie made him think that she was a grandchild. She had to be Fay's.

On the jetty old men jigged for squid with their heads lowered against the wind. Dyson stood out there looking across at the yacht club and the rusty roofs of Cockleshell on the farther shore.

Fay Keenan. He hadn't even considered that she might still be in town. Hadn't she left long before him? He had anticipated some awkward encounters. There would be the people he'd gone to school with, the ones who always talked of shooting through to the city at the first opportunity but never actually left. He prepared himself for their prickly defensiveness, consoling himself in the knowledge that after ten years these meetings would only be momentary. Most people would settle for a wave in the street, a brief greeting in Woolworths. But he hadn't considered folks like the Keenans. They were full-on people. They were salt of the earth. They would never settle for just a meeting on the main drag.

And Fay. With a daughter. He hadn't considered that at all.

For a few days Dyson kept to the house. He only went out to take Ricky to school and collect him afterwards. All day he absorbed himself in little projects of household repair and modification. He told himself it was the rain that kept him at bay but in truth he had the jitters. He was back to feeling that weird, diffuse guilt which had dogged him all his life. He'd given up teasing that one out years ago. The old man's early death, the disappointment he was to his mother, the business with Fay. And, God knows, the unravelling of Sophie. It was old news but ever fresh in him. The way he'd jumped, blushing already, when Marjorie Keenan called his name.

With Ricky beside him, he lay awake at night with real misgivings about coming home. Irony he could deal with, but the complications of history might be another matter.

On the third day, in the early afternoon, Marjorie Keenan came knocking as he knew she would. Come for dinner tonight, she told him. She had a lamb leg big as a guitar. There was no way out.

The Keenans lived down by the surf beach in a shabby art deco place beneath Norfolk Island pines. Dyson arrived at six and stood for a moment at the door, bracing himself for the necessary explanations about his status as a single parent. Ricky looped his fingers around Dyson's belt. Both looked up at the soughing pines before Dyson knocked.

Marjorie squeezed each of them on the doorstep and dragged them indoors. The house was unchanged since the days he'd come here to play pool and grope their daughter furtively in the garage. In the hallway a candle burned before an icon of a severe Russian Christ. There were seascapes on the walls and a portrait of the Pope. The place smelled of meat and potatoes and the strange lemony odour of old people. Somewhere in the house a television blared.

In the kitchen Don Keenan rose on sticks and met Dyson with a hand outstretched, copper bracelet gleaming. There were tears in his eyes.

Look at you, he said. Lord, just look at you.

Long time, Don.

The old man sat and wiped his face. Yeah, he said brightly. And time wounds all heels, eh?

Except that it's his knees that've given out, said Marjorie. That's a lifetime of football for you.

They beckoned him to sit and Ricky edged onto his lap, reserved but curious. Dyson saw that the boy was transfixed by the old man. The tears, the florid cheeks, the Brylcreemed hair, the walking sticks. Ricky curled against his father. Dyson smelled the sweetness of his scalp.

Mister Keenan was my coach, Rick. When I was a boy. He was a gun footballer, you know. Played for Claremont. Three hundred and twenty-two games for Railways – that's a team here.

You like footy, Ricky? the old man asked.

The boy nodded.

Who's your favourite player, then?

Ricky looked at his father.

Go on, said Dyson.

Leaper, said the boy.

Ah, said Don. Now *he* can play!

Lamb's ready, said Marjorie.

Still cooking on the woodstove, said Dyson admiringly. Look at the size of that thing.

It's the Rolls-Royce of ranges, that, she said.

Big as a blessed Rolls-Royce, too, said Don.

Just as their plates came and the old man was carving the meat, the thin blonde child came into the kitchen and took a seat.

You met Sky, said Marjorie.

Sky, said Dyson. This is Ricky.

Hi, the girl murmured.

Lo, said Ricky.

There was a brief moment of bewilderment when grace was said. After all the crossing and amens Ricky glanced at Dyson for reassurance. Then hunger got the better of him and he ate unselfconsciously.

The talk was of the town, how the harbour had finally been cleaned up and the whales had returned and brought new tourists to the place. There are wineries now, said Don, and good wine like this one. Dyson didn't have the heart to tell him he'd given up the booze but he knew that

Marjorie wouldn't have missed the fact that his glass was untouched. The food was simple and hearty and the kitchen sleepy-warm. It was nice to be with them again after all this time. The Keenans were good people and he felt bad that he'd left it so long to come and see them. After all, he'd been closer to them at one stage than he was to his own mother. A long time had passed since the business with him and Fay. He told himself he needn't have been so anxious.

Ricky pleased Marjorie by taking a second helping of everything. Rain lashed the windows and though he was sober Dyson felt as safe as a man with four drinks under his belt. Eventually the kids sloped off shyly to watch TV. Marjorie made a pot of Irish breakfast.

You don't need to explain about your wife, Peter, said the old woman, pouring him a cup. We know already. We'll spare you that.

News travels fast, he murmured, stung.

Small town, mate, said Don. Don't we know all about that.

Well, said Dyson, doing his best to recover. That pretty much explains why I'm back.

There was a long, hesitant silence. From the loungeroom up the hall came the antic noise of a cartoon. Dyson wondered if that huge ruined sofa was still there in front of the TV. A lifetime ago, on the same cracked upholstery, he felt the hot weight of a girl's breasts in his hands for the first time, and it was odd to think of Ricky and Sky up there.

Sky, he said. She's Fay's?

They nodded.

Staying with you for a while?

Oh, said Marjorie with a tired smile. We've had Sky on and off for years. Most of her life, I spose.

Ah, said Dyson.

Well, said the old man. Like you, Fay's had her troubles.

She doesn't live in town?

No. She's been all over.

In trying to mask his relief, Dyson scalded his mouth with tea.

We thought of suing for permanent custody for the child's sake, said the old man. But it's a dead loss. Welfare and the courts – it's all about the rights of the mother no matter what.

Anyway, said Marjorie with a forced cheeriness that made it plain she'd cut Don off before he got into his stride. It's worked out well just going along the way we have, unofficially. Things are coming good in the end. Fay and you are in the same sort of boat in a way. You know, recovering. In fact it's amazing you're here, Peter, because Fay's due here any day. Maybe you two can catch up.

Well, said Dyson in alarm. To be honest I'm not—

It's been very hard for us, Peter, said the old lady. Life doesn't turn out how you plan it. And it's difficult when you're old, when you think that your job's done and you can rest a little.

You're not prepared for dealing with the kinds of things we've had to deal with, to live through.

Stinking, filthy bloody drugs—

Don.

She's abandoned a child, said the old man. She's stolen anything we've ever had. We've spent all our savings on treatments and debts and she's brought thugs and crims into our home and frightened the tripe out of her mother. She's put us through a living hell.

But, said Marjorie emphatically, we have our precious Sky. And we're past the worst and we forgive and forget. Don't we, Don?

Yes, said the old man subsiding, contrite, in his chair.

And we're grateful for small mercies.

Dyson drank his tea. His mouth felt scoured now. A junkie, he thought. You couldn't honestly be surprised. It would explain the rash of calls a couple of years ago, the breathless messages on the machine.

We always loved you, Peter, said Marjorie.

Loved you as our own, said Don. Gawd, we even thought you'd be family in the end.

She needs safe friends, said Marjorie. Clean friends. She's putting her life back together.

And we need a break, son. Now and then. Just a blessed rest.

You're a good person, Peter. Say you'll think about it. Say you'll come and see her.

Dyson felt the heat of the stove in his bones. He looked at their ravaged faces. And rain peppered the window.

Dyson had no desire to see Fay Keenan. When she called that time he did not respond to her messages. He bore her no ill will but he did fear the force of her personality. The intervening years had not diminished his memory of the time, almost the entirety of his high school life, that he'd spent in her thrall. They began as fumbling fourteen-year-olds when he was her father's most promising player and she was the flashy captain of the girls' hockey team. They were a major item, a school scandal, infamous for their declarations of eternal love and the heroics of their lust. By the age of sixteen the love was gone but the lust lived on in a kind of mutual self-loathing. Their relationship had boiled down to a futile addiction, a form of entertainment for their classmates who saw them as a bad show which refused to go off the air.

Dyson's mother disliked Fay but the Keenans took to him. To the Keenans Fay and him were just two talented kids taking life by the throat. What they didn't seem to see was how strange and pathological the whole affair became. How these kids isolated themselves in their passion until they became friendless and obsessed. They didn't see them destroying each other. As a boy Dyson relished the warmth of the Keenan home and although the Catholic business mystified him, he recognized them as people of virtue and kindness, even forgiveness. By comparison his own mother seemed dry and inflexible. She looked down on the Keenans because Don worked for the railways. Dyson came to love them and in later years, when it was all over, he wondered if the whole grisly thing had lasted so long because he liked to be around the Keenans as much as their daughter. But that was just sentimental. What kept Fay and him together was sex. It was a habit only catastrophe could break.

Right from the outset there was something mesmerizing about Fay Keenan. She had a cockiness, an impulsive brio that was exciting. Dyson was never a courageous boy. Even in football he was talented but weak-willed. The coach's daughter had real guts. She was so pretty, so lithe, with a wicked laugh under all that blonde hair. Fay was smart, too. At school she coasted shamelessly. Her parents were convinced that she was destined for medicine or the law. She could really talk up a storm. Yet in the end Dyson hardly heard anything she said; he settled for the curve of her neck, the heat of her mouth, the spill of her hair across his body, and even when all they had to say to one another was carping ugliness, he was too well-fed, too passive, too lazy to break it off and move on. For the last two years of school they were miserable. They had their disaster and Fay failed her exams. They were just another small-town story. And in the way of such stories they met years later, stoned at a Christmas barbecue in the city, and screwed in a potting shed from which they staggered full of regret and recrimination.

It was so tawdry that it should have been comical, but Dyson could only see the damage they'd done each other.

A week after his dinner with the Keenans, Dyson took Ricky and a boy from his class out to Jacky's Bridge to fish for bream after school. The boys were new friends and still shy with one another and right from the start it was clear that the fishing idea was a dud. He didn't know what it was. Maybe they were too young or fresh to each other for the stillness required, but within ten minutes they were restless standing out there on the bank so he packed the gear and led them up to the bridge itself.

This is boring, said the other boy, Jared.

Yeah, said Ricky faintly, treading a line between solidarity and mutiny.

Well, you'll think differently in a minute, said Dyson. Here, climb up between these big posts. See these little flat bits? Lie there. Here, I'll show you.

Dyson crawled up beneath the supports of the wooden bridge and lay on his back in the moist gravel so he could look up at the sky slatted through the timbers. Sceptically, the boys joined him. He sensed that he was about to make a fool of himself and shame Ricky by association but he didn't have a better idea to entertain them with. He was also suddenly mindful that this was something he'd discovered with Fay. There was such a long list of local things he couldn't dissociate from her; she was there at every turn.

Dad? murmured Ricky, embarrassed.

Stay down. I can hear something coming.

The boys fidgeted beside him. Jared smelled of Plasticine or something else slightly musty. He was, very distinctly, a stranger, someone else's child.

Just then a semi broached the bend and Dyson began to laugh in anticipation. Within seconds the truck was on the bridge and the piles and sleepers roared. Spikes spat and rattled and the dirt beneath them shook. Dyson began to yell. It startled the boys a second until his voice was swallowed up by the great, hot shadow that passed overhead.

Hey, said Jared quietly in the aftermath. Cool.

For another half hour they lay there waiting, giggling, yelling and laughing themselves to the point of hiccups.

As she took delivery of her muddy son, Jared's mother seemed brazenly curious about Dyson. He stood blushing on her verandah as she sized him up. It seemed that word was out on him. He wondered if it was his apparent availability or his wife's suicide that interested her. Either way he didn't linger.

It was almost dark when they got home. The harbour lights were on, the jetties pretty in a way that they could never be in daylight. Dyson was only halfway out of the car before he saw a shadow on the verandah and then the glow of a cigarette. He knew it would be her. Ricky pressed against him as they mounted the steps.

Just me, said Fay.

Her face was little more than a white dab in the gloom.

Fay, he murmured.

Didn't mean to startle anybody.

That's okay.

First ciggie I've ever smoked on your mum's verandah, that's for sure.

Dyson found the lock and opened the house. He hesitated a moment before switching on the porchlight and when he did Fay seemed to cringe beneath it. Her face was pale, her hair without lustre.

It's getting chilly, he said. You'd better come in.

I can't stay.

No. Fair enough.

Dyson tried to understand what he was feeling. It was so strange to see her again. She blew smoke from the side of her mouth, the way she always had, and tossed the butt out into the yard.

This is your little boy.

Ricky, said Dyson.

Your dad and me, Fay said with an attempt at brightness. We went to school together.

Ricky licked his lips. Dyson ushered him inside toward the bathroom and stood in the doorway.

Mum told me about your wife.

Oh, he asked, startled. She did?

I'm sorry to hear it.

Well.

And she told you about me, I imagine.

A bit. She didn't elaborate. I met Sky.

Isn't she great?

Yeah. She looks like you.

So Mum didn't give you the gory details.

No.

God bless her.

Well, he said. She's a trouper.

Dyson tried to look past Fay to the harbour lights and the navy sky still tinted by the vanished sun, but even thin and wan as she was in the unflattering light, she had a compelling presence. The cargo pants and jumper hung off her and her lips were chapped. She seemed wrung out, chastened, even. Yet she took up all the available space out there on the verandah.

For some reason I wanted to tell you myself, she said looking him straight in the face, her arms folded across her breasts. Once I found out you were home I had to explain myself. We go back so far, you and me. I didn't want you finding out from someone else.

Sure, he said uncertainly.

Funny, you know. I've had to give up worrying about what people think anymore. Burnt all the bridges. But with you . . . it's different.

It shouldn't be. Fay, we don't even know each other. I don't mean to be . . . but we were kids.

And here you are.

Dyson folded his arms.

I was in rehab, Pete. I'm six months clean.

That's good. That's great.

I fucked up. Been fuckin up for years.

You don't have to talk about this, Dyson said, hearing water purl into the bath up the hallway.

But I want to. Maybe you don't wanna hear it.

I've got Ricky to get through the bath, he said. The hot water.

Yeah.

Maybe you'd better come in?

No. It's alright.

Can . . . can I do anything for you?

Like, why am I here? she said with a wry smile, eyes glittering.

It's just that I'm not that steady yet, myself. You know? I don't know what I can offer you.

I need a friend, that's all.

Dyson sighed, torn.

I know it'll be hard to trust me.

Fay.

I'm supposed to seek out good people. But it's alright. I understand. I'll see you.

Chilled and miserable, he let her walk down into the dark while behind him water pounded into the bath. He hadn't even let her tell him what it was that she was addicted to; he didn't even offer her that kindness. But how could he tell her that he wasn't as uncomplicatedly good as she imagined? How could he be honest with her and say that he was afraid of her and afraid of his own reactions, frightened of lapsing into old habits? Self-preservation – did it ever feel anything but ugly?

He pushed the door to and switched off the porchlight.

In the morning, bleary and unrested, he came upon Fay outside the school gate. He supposed that for a while at least such meetings would be inevitable. And then one day she'd be gone again. The sky hung low and dark. There was a bitter wind from the south. Fay wore a huge stretched jumper that looked like one of Don's and she hugged herself as she turned to him.

Haven't done that for a while, she murmured.

Bring her to school?

I think she was embarrassed.

Ah.

Hurts, she said fishing out a fag. But I spose I deserve it.

Dyson walked uphill, careful not to hurry, and she fell into step beside him.

Sorry about last night.

Well, he murmured. Me too.

Out over the sea a storm brewed. The air in its path felt pure and steely. Dyson couldn't help feel that Fay's cigarette was an offence against such clarity. In even thinking it he was, he knew, his mother's son, but that did not make it less true.

How's your folks? he asked.

Good. But I don't know how long I can live with them. They want me to stay a while but nobody's naming dates. I'm kind of on probation with Sky. And with them, I spose. They won't give her up easily. Not that I blame them. They've been good to me. Dad used to drive three hundred miles every fortnight to visit me in rehab. They've been great, you know, but I think I'll go mad if I stay too long.

Where would you go? he asked.

Oh, I'll stay in town. Rent somewhere close so they can all see each other. Sky needs them now. She knows I'm a fuck-up so she'll need reassurance. I have fantasies about a little house on one of those old dairy farms out along the coast.

Something clear and clean, somewhere I can start again from scratch. You know what I mean?

Yeah, he said. I do.

But there's nowhere you can really *do* that. Everywhere you go there'll be some link. A bit of history. Anyway, I'm broke. Need a job but still feel a bit too ginger to cope with the stress.

I understand.

But in the meantime I'm going nuts. Jesus, I thought rehab was tough. I've got Mum watching me like a hawk and Sky expecting me to piss off at any moment. And the old man desperately trying not to spew out all his resentment and scare me off.

I spose it'll take time.

She sniffed angrily. Yeah. Time.

They came to his street and paused a moment.

You ever see any of the old crew? she said.

No, he murmured. To be honest I can hardly remember anybody else.

Scary.

He shrugged.

Well, she said. I'll leave you alone. Don't worry.

Dyson arranged his mouth to speak but found nothing to say.

Looks like I'm still trouble, she murmured. For you at least.

Did he imagine it or was there really a tiny twist of satisfaction to Fay's mouth as she said this, a thread of pride in knowing that she had a lingering influence over him?

He mumbled goodbye and walked home in the same turmoil that he'd stewed in all night. How could you help someone like Fay? How could you trust her? If it wasn't the drugs it was the old thrill of the power that she wielded. He just wasn't strong or confident enough to battle it right now. Wasn't his first responsibility to Ricky, to his own sanity? He had his own problems to deal with. Yet he felt like such a bloodless bastard and so disloyal to Don and Marjorie after all their years of kindness. He'd all but grown up in their home and here he was refusing to help their daughter. And that poor, wary little girl. How could he live with himself?

Rain fell all day. He sat inside with a fire burning, the household chores mounting up around him. It was the kind of day you could feel descending upon you, when you drag everything out and hash it over once again despite yourself. When you looked back at Sophie and the pregnancy, wondering what signs you missed. The precious time it cost after the birth before you realized something was badly wrong, before you finally spoke, acted, asked. And the dozens of times when you didn't hear, when you reacted clumsily, said and did the wrong thing. The drowning weight of it.

There were times, even while she was alive, when Dyson questioned his attraction to Sophie. They met in his early years of teaching. She was a physiotherapist with dark, short hair and green eyes. Any stranger could take a look at Ricky and see what Dyson had seen in his mother. They shared the same smooth, olive skin and vanilla scent. Sophie exuded a seriousness of purpose that some people thought solemn. He loved her calm trust and the simple delight that lit up her face. Once, even before she got sick and everything began to seem forced and provisional, he allowed himself the bitter possibility that he may have fallen in love with Sophie from sheer relief that she wasn't Fay Keenan. Because when they met he was still raw. And there Sophie was, pretty, considered, dependable, a sanctuary from the narcissistic and mercurial. He did love her. But it gnawed at him then, as now, that he might have loved the safety of her above all else. Maybe she knew it all along. It was a nasty thought, because if she did then he could not truly console himself with the doctors' talk of chemical imbalance and postnatal depression. She would have had plenty to be miserable about, and he would have to wear some blame for her misery and maybe even her death. Even the weak are

41

cruel in their way. You couldn't cling to victim-
hood all your life.

The fire was so bright in the hearth that even
at the brink of despair he found himself finally
and mercifully anaesthetized before it. As he sat
there into the afternoon it sucked the air from
the room and danced before him like a thought
just out of reach.

He woke to a banging at the door and when he
staggered up from the couch Fay was at the window. He opened the door. Ricky stood looking
up at him with frank curiosity.

Rick. Hell. I fell asleep.

So we see, said Fay wryly.

Damn. But thanks for bringing him, Fay.

I know the way, said Ricky.

Yes, mate. Course you do.

Dad, said the boy holding up a sheet of
butcher's paper. Look at my picture.

Dyson took the crumpled painting and held it away from him to see it. Jacky's Bridge! he said.

Here's me. Here's you.

Of course. And what about Jared?

Aw, I forgot him.

Dyson smiled. He looked up and saw Fay smiling too. Then he noticed Sky standing out on the steps in the drizzling rain.

You're all wet, he said. You better come in. Hey Rick, let's get some towels.

The fire was almost out but the house was still warm. Dyson towelled his son dry and watched Sky submit to the care of her mother. It was painful, the selfconsciousness of it. Outside the rain intensified, the day darkened.

I can't believe I slept through, he said.

Things happen, said Fay.

I'll drive you home.

No, it's okay.

It's pouring.

Fay shook her head.

You'll get drenched.

There were tears in Fay's eyes. Dyson stood there confounded. The kids wandered over to the kitchen window to see water spill from the iron tank outside.

He's got a cubbyhouse, said Sky over her shoulder in a tone of accusation.

My Dad made it, said Ricky.

Dyson removed the booster seat so Fay could sit in the front of the car beside him. He made sure the kids were buckled up before he eased them all out into the deluge.

I had a blue with Dad, said Fay. He wanted to drive us, I wanted to walk. Well, I'd rather drive but I've lost my licence. Stupid, stupid.

Spose you just want some independence.

Life in a cleft stick, eh.

Dyson drove them out toward the beach where little weatherboard cottages seemed to cower under the downpour.

God, this rain.

Thought you hated winter, she said. What a joke, coming back here, then.

Over the tin roofs the sea was steely-smooth and the Norfolk Island pines rose like a stockade against the south.

That painting, Fay said. That was our bridge, right?

He nodded. They coasted in to the Keenans' place.

I won't tell them, she murmured.

Tell them what?

That you slept through.

Thanks for collecting him for me.

Can't have them thinking you left a child in the rain.

Bye, Fay.

Already Marjorie was on the porch unfurling an umbrella in preparation for their rescue. He could imagine old Don out there trolling the streets for them right now. He honked the horn as he pulled away.

On Saturday morning Dyson drove out along the coast with a pair of binoculars to show Ricky the humpbacks coursing their way towards the tropics, and for a while they stood on a headland as a whale and her calf lolled in the clear, sunlit water at their feet. The boy was enchanted. Vapour and spray rose around them. The crash of tails whacking the surface resonated in their own skin and hair. They hooted like sportsfans until the show was over. Heading homeward, with Ricky still euphoric, Dyson thought about the whaling station, now a museum, on the out-skirts of town. He figured he'd let that keep a while. For now the boy was alight with wonder. Why dash that excitement with cold, nasty history right at the outset?

As they came back into town Ricky spotted the football oval and rose in his seat.

Dad, can we kick the footy?

The sun was out, there was a ball in the back

of the car. Dyson wheeled them in to park beside the other cars around the boundary. A junior game was in recess so they dashed out to the western goal square and punted the ball up and back between the posts. While Ricky capered solemnly around the turf, Dyson took in the twelve-year-olds in their team huddles on the flank. Nothing had changed in thirty years – the coach's harangue, the half-sucked orange quarters on the grass, the fat and hungover parents nursing their breakfast meatpie and fag.

Dad, watch this! Frank Leaper snaps on goal!

Ricky hooked the ball across his shoulder. The kick fell short but Dyson ushered it across the line.

A car horn blared.

Through! cried Ricky.

Six points, Dyson said.

The horn went again: shave-and-a-haircut-ten-cents. Dyson looked over. Don Keenan waved from the wheel of his ancient Holden.

Out in the centre the umpire blew his whistle

for the resumption of play and the teams straggled back out onto the park. Ricky whined and baulked at having to vacate the goal square but Dyson herded him back to the sidelines. They drew up beside the old man's car.

Got a bit of a kick on him, said Don Keenan.

How are you, Don?

The old man shrugged. What doesn't kill you makes you older. Know anythin about addiction?

A few things, I spose, said Dyson leaning against the old HT as two boys flew for the bouncedown. The ball shied out to a solitary kid who was so stunned to have possession of it that he stood motionless until run down by the pack.

Thanks for takin an interest in Fay. It means a lot to us.

Dyson said nothing.

We're just about at our wits' end, said Don. No parent should have to see the things I've seen.

She's trying, said Dyson.

You got that right.

The ball soared, spiralling into the sun.

But we love her, said Don. You understand that, don't you?

Dyson said he did.

Late Sunday night, when Ricky was long abed and the fire all but out, there was a gentle knock at the door.

I'm sorry, Fay murmured. I just had to.

He let her in and with her came the night chill. They sat by the hearth but he didn't stoke the fire for fear of encouraging Fay to linger. She sat down in a quilted jacket, jeans and hiking boots and fingered the book he'd been reading. As she leant in toward the remains of the fire her hair crowded her face.

Everything alright?

She shook her head.

He sighed. Want a cuppa?

Yeah, she said. Coffee.

He went into the kitchen to fill the kettle.

When he returned Fay was putting wood on the fire.

I should have been at a meeting tonight, she said. I've skipped two in a row.

So don't miss the next one.

There's no one I can turn to, Pete. You're it.

Your parents know you're here?

Yeah. They're freaking. When . . . when I get agitated and restless like this they think I'm gonna go out and score.

And are you?

I'm here aren't I? Shit, they're still searching my room and I'm thirty years old, for Chrissake. Least if I'm here they'll relax. God, they're ecstatic. You're the Golden Boy. Dad even drove me, she said with a girlish laugh.

He drove you here?

So fucking sad.

Dyson lowered himself into a chair and felt a new weight of fatigue on him.

Tell me about your wife, she said.

What kind of state are you in, Fay?

Frazzled, she said. Teetering. So tell me about her.

Dyson shook his head. Fay whistled through her teeth.

What do you want from me? he asked.

Respect, she said. No. Adoration. Shit, Pete, I just want a safe place to be. Someone trust-worthy. I can trust you, can't I?

Fay pulled her knees up to her chin and in that single movement, with her hair down her arms and her eyes tilted up at him, she became an eerie ghost of her teenage self. Dyson got up and went back to the kitchen to make her coffee. He stood, shaken, at the stove. He turned a teaspoon over and over in his hand so that the light caught it.

You didn't answer me, Fay said in the door-way.

I don't know the answer.

Can't trust yourself, you mean.

Jesus, Fay, what is it that you really want?

I dunno, she said arching against the door-frame. Just now? Comfort, I spose. A few of the edges taken off. This fucking town – I shouldn't have come back.

So why did you?

I want my kid.

Dyson felt hemmed in now. He was revolted by her. He couldn't help it. All that restless will, the cruelty of it made him sick.

What are you thinking? she asked. Your face went black. What're you thinking about me?

Nothing, Fay.

I used to be a prize once. I was a trophy and you had me.

Let's go and sit by the fire, he said. Here's your coffee.

You're uncomfortable.

Yes.

I came here for comfort and you're uncomfortable, she said, her face flushed.

I don't think there's any comfort I can give you.

The simple pleasures, she said, lifting the mug to her mouth.

Maybe you should go.

You don't understand what I've been through!

And I'm rapidly losing interest in finding out.

You don't know what's been taken from me, what I've given up. It's inhuman. No one should have to go through what I've been through.

The blood was in her face now. Her eyes glittered. She was beautiful again.

Fay—

Jesus, I'm aching. I need love.

Your family—

I need more!

You'll meet good people, he said. It's a slow road.

I can't wait. Can't you see, I can't wait.

Think of Sky.

Don't do that to me, she said. Look down your nose, turn me away, lecture me. I really thought you were a friend.

I am, he murmured, and as he did so he knew it was a lie.

She dragged her hair back off her face and wiped her eyes. You can't even spare me a hug?

Dyson felt such a shit. He sighed and looked at her, relenting. Sensing it, she smiled.

Let's go to bed, Pete.

He froze even as he reached for her. Fay, you really should go.

What harm can it do?

Fay—

I can't drink, can't drive, can't live in my own place, can't do Mr Speed. Jesus, I can't upset Mum and Dad. A mercy fuck isn't against the law, Pete, it's not a blow against the Higher Power. Hello, my name's Fay Keenan and I'm desperate—

Stop it.

You used to beg me.

Please keep your voice down.

I can't believe you!

Well you'd better believe it.

It's so humiliating, she said beginning to weep.

I'm coming apart here and you're just . . . just watching?

Fay, you'll wake Ricky.

I don't give a shit.

Just calm down.

She wiped her face with the sleeve of her baggy jumper. A glistening trail of snot and tears lay on the wool and Dyson stared at it while his mind raced.

You won't even hold me, will you?

No, he murmured. I'm sorry, but I can't.

I don't think we were ever friends.

You're probably right, he said. We were obsessed, caught up in something. Too young. We were children. We did damage.

Fay gulped at her coffee. She looked at him carefully as though taking his measure. She was beautiful. Any man would want her. She'd taste of coffee and cigarettes and tears and her hair would fall around you like a curtain.

You have no idea how my parents adore you, said Fay. I could have hated you for being in town when I came home. My big moment. Nothing I've done in the past six months to put my life right could impress them the way you did by simply arriving unchanged of old. And you know what? Stolen thunder and all, I was glad. Happy for them, happy for me. We really thought you'd be there for us.

I appreciate that, he said. But I don't think they expect me to sleep with you.

They don't know how cold and dead inside you really are.

That's probably true, he admitted, exhausted now.

You know they never did find out about our little secret. God knows, every other shitty thing I ever did somehow got back to them, but they never even suspected that. Two days shy of seventeen. And your fuckin mother paid for it.

Oh, Fay.

You know how my parents are. You know what it'd do to them. It'd crush them. Break their hearts.

Don't.

And you, the tin god. They could blame you for everything that's ever happened to me, everything I've put em through.

Dyson went cold. He held on to the bench and stared at her. God, how thoroughly she saw through him. He never really knew if Fay regretted the abortion they'd obtained all those years ago, but she gauged him well enough to sense how it ate at him. And she knew where his real vanity lay, what it would cost him to be reviled by her parents. When Fay took off to leave them in the lurch again, how could he live here in town with them, meeting them at the school gate every morning? What would he be to them, then, the killer of their unborn grandchild?

Pete, if I leave this house and go down to the trawlers and score tonight, what're you gonna tell them? That you turned me away? Ruined my recovery like you ruined me before?

Did I, though? he murmured. Ruin you. Is that how it was?

She laughed and put the mug on the bench.

There was a thud from the livingroom and Fay turned, startled.

Ricky? she called.

Dyson slipped past her and saw a log fallen out onto the hearth. A plume of smoke rose in the room and he kicked the smouldering wood back into the grate. He leant on the mantle to get control of himself.

Fay stood in the middle of the room waving smoke away. Her manic mood had broken.

So that's a no, then?

It's a no, Fay. Regardless.

It's blackmail, she said. I know.

It's vicious.

You think I'd do it? she asked, smiling. You think I'd tell them?

No, he whispered prayerfully. Because you love them. I think you love your daughter. You've come too far, Fay. Too much self-respect.

Dyson wondered if it might be true, whether she had any pity in her at all.

Well, said Fay. I spose we'll see, won't we?

Yes, Dyson said turning back to the smoulder-ing log in the grate. I guess we will.

He kept his back to her.

The door shut so quietly that he had to turn around to see that she was gone.

PICADOR SHOTS

SHALOM AUSLANDER
'Holocaust Tips for Kids' and 'Smite the Heathens,
Charlie Brown' from *Beware of God*

CRAIG DAVIDSON
'A Mean Utility' and 'Life in the Flesh' from *Rust and Bone*

BRET EASTON ELLIS
'Water from the Sun' and 'Discovering Japan'
from *The Informers*

NELL FREUDENBERGER
'Lucky Girls' from *Lucky Girls*

ALEKSANDAR HEMON
'Exchange of Pleasant Words' and 'A Coin'
from *The Question of Bruno*

JACKIE KAY
'Sonata' from *Wish I Was Here*

MATTHEW KNEALE
'Powder' from *Small Crimes in An Age of Abundance*

CLAIRE MESSUD
'The Professor's History'

JAMES SALTER
'My Lord You' and 'Palm Court' from *Last Night*

COLM TÓIBÍN
'The Use of Reason' from *Mothers and Sons*

NIALL WILLIAMS
unpublished new story – 'The Unrequited'

TIM WINTON
'Small Mercies' from *The Turning*

All collections are available in Picador.